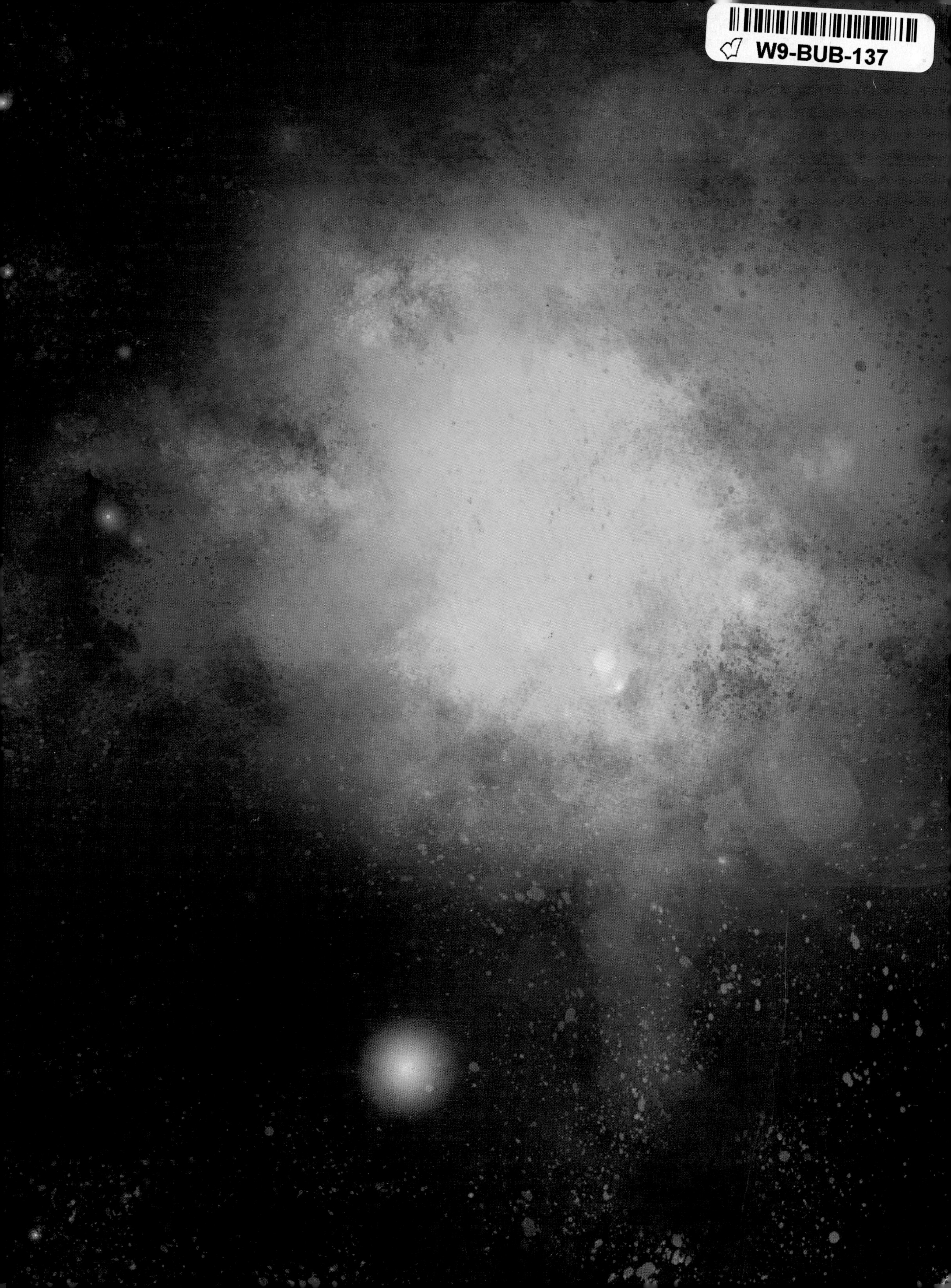

CAPTAIN RAPTOR

and the PERILOUS PLANET

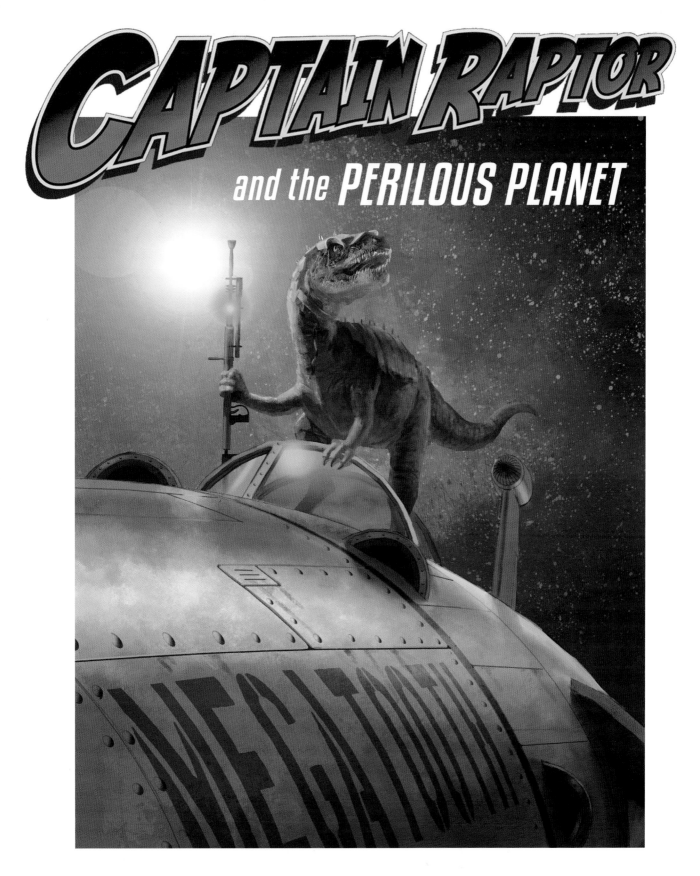

KEVIN O'MALLEY and PATRICK O'BRIEN
Illustrated by PATRICK O'BRIEN

Charlesbridge

ON THE OUTER EDGE OF THE ERRATUS ASTEROID BELT, THE MIGHTY SPACESHIP **MEGATOOTH** CRUISES, READY FOR ACTION.

CAPTAIN RAPTOR AND HIS CREW ARE HARD AT WORK ON A NEW FORCE-FIELD SHIELDING SYSTEM.

LIEUTENANT THREETOE MAPS ANOTHER SLOW RUN THROUGH THE BELT.

PROFESSOR ANGLEOPTEROUS HAPPILY TINKERS WITH HIS NEW SHIELDING SYSTEM.

"STARTING SHIELD TEST NUMBER 215. ISN'T THIS EXCITING, CAPTAIN?"

"ABSOLUTELY THRILLING, PROFESSOR," SIGHS THE CAPTAIN.

IT'S SLOW WORK FOR A DINOSAUR WHO **LIVES FOR ACTION.**

SUDDENLY COMMUNICATIONS SPECIALIST SPIKEBACK LOOKS UP FROM HIS STATION. "WE'RE GETTING A CALL ON THE EMERGENCY SPACE BEACON SYSTEM. IT'S SOMEONE NAMED COMMANDER BROCK OF THE PLANET MAMMALIA. BUT I CAN BARELY HEAR HIM."

"PUT HIM ON-SCREEN, SPIKEBACK," SAYS CAPTAIN RAPTOR.

"CAPTAIN RAPTOR, ARE YOU THERE? ...

... LAVA IS RISING ...

... AN ERUPTION ON PLANET PYROS PRIME ...

... WE'RE ON OUR WAY ... RESCUE THEM ... CAN'T MAKE IT IN TIME ..."

... RESEARCH SCIENTISTS TRAPPED IN MOUNT BLEAK ...

"WE'VE LOST HIS SIGNAL, CAPTAIN."

"LIEUTENANT THREETOE, **TOP SPEED TO PYROS PRIME!**" THUNDERS CAPTAIN RAPTOR.

"ALL HANDS ON THE COMMAND DECK!"

"PROFESSOR, TELL ME—WHAT DO WE KNOW ABOUT THE PLANET?"

"PYROS PRIME IS REMARKABLY UNSTABLE. IF THE LARGEST VOLCANO ERUPTS, THE ENTIRE PLANET WILL EXPLODE IN JUST MINUTES," EXPLAINS PROFESSOR ANGLEOPTEROUS. "WE NEED TO GET THOSE SCIENTISTS TO SAFETY!"

"CAPTAIN," SAYS THREETOE, "READINGS SHOW THE PLANET IS BEING **BOMBARDED** BY ASTEROIDS. I'M NOT SURE THE SHIP CAN TAKE IT."

"PROFESSOR, GET THAT SHIELD OF YOURS WORKING," SAYS CAPTAIN RAPTOR. "WE'RE IN FOR A ROUGH WELCOME!"

THE *MEGATOOTH* DODGES LEFT AND RIGHT AS IT ENTERS THE UPPER ATMOSPHERE OF PYROS PRIME. SUDDENLY THE SHIP IS **STRUCK** BY A **FLAMING BALL** OF MOLTEN ROCK.

WHAM!

"STABILIZERS ARE UNRESPONSIVE, CAPTAIN!" YELLS THREETOE.

"TRANSFER CONTROL TO ME!" SHOUTS CAPTAIN RAPTOR. "GRAB ON TO SOMETHING, FOLKS. THIS IS GOING TO BE ONE *WILD RIDE!*"

COULD THIS BE *THE END* OF CAPTAIN RAPTOR?

"BRACE FOR IMPACT!"
BELLOWS CAPTAIN RAPTOR.

THE *MEGATOOTH* **SKIDS AND JUMPS** ACROSS THE GROUND LIKE A STONE ACROSS A POND.

IT COMES TO REST AT THE BASE OF MOUNT BLEAK, ITS TAIL CONTROLS **BADLY DAMAGED.**

"OK, PROFESSOR," ORDERS CAPTAIN RAPTOR, "GET THIS BIRD FIXED AND READY TO FLY. THREETOE, FIND ME THE BEST WAY OFF THIS ROCK."

"SPIKEBACK, KEEP THE RADIO OPEN AND LET ME KNOW IF THERE'S ANY TROUBLE. I'M GOING TO FIND THOSE SCIENTISTS."

CAPTAIN RAPTOR FIGHTS HIS WAY THROUGH THE STEAMY JUNGLE. THE GROUND IS HOT AND SLICK BENEATH HIS FEET.

A LOUD SLITHERING SOUND SUDDENLY FILLS THE AIR.

SSSSSSSSSSSSS!

COBRASAURUS!

THE GREAT VENOM-FANGED REPTILE DIVES STRAIGHT AT HIM!

COULD *THIS* BE THE END OF CAPTAIN RAPTOR?

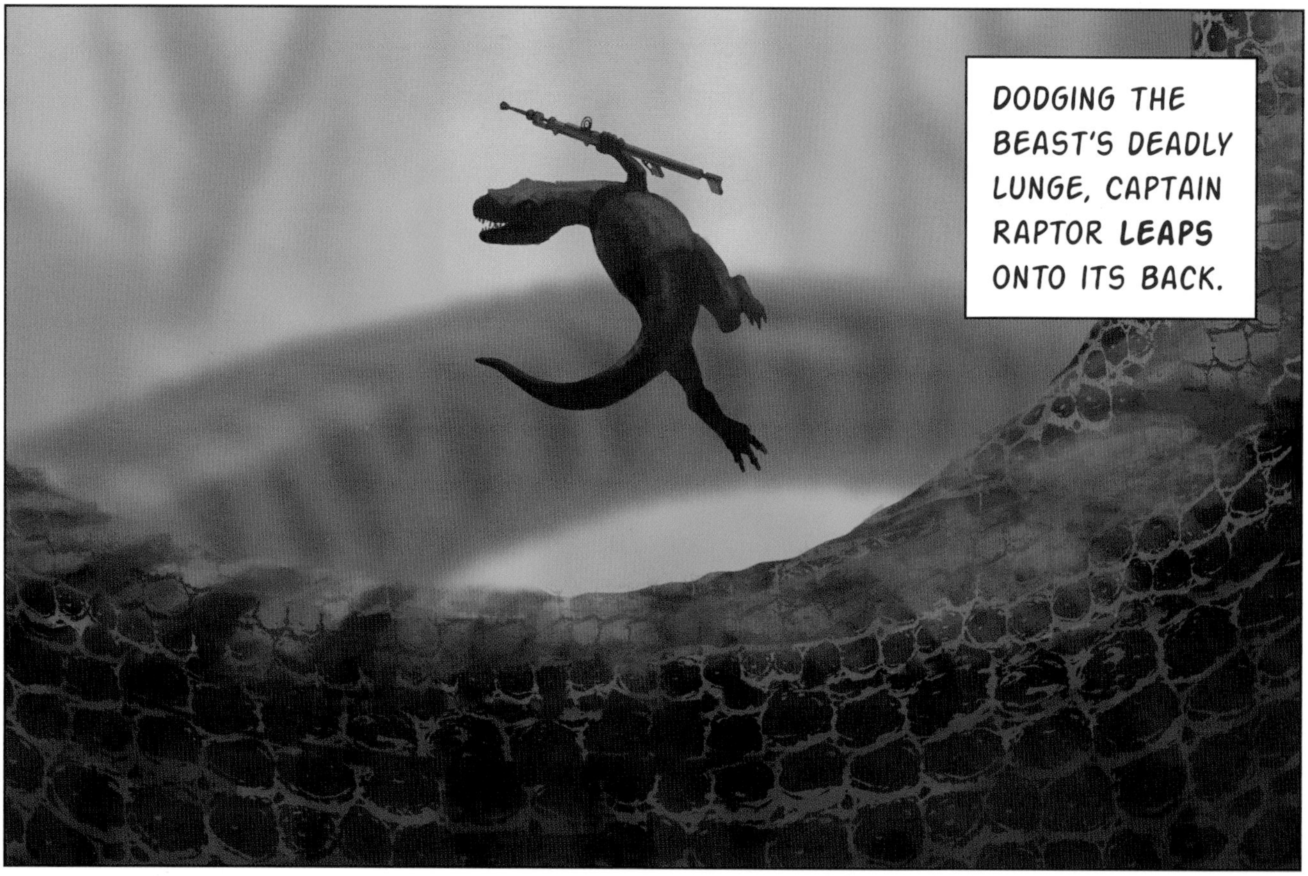
DODGING THE BEAST'S DEADLY LUNGE, CAPTAIN RAPTOR **LEAPS** ONTO ITS BACK.

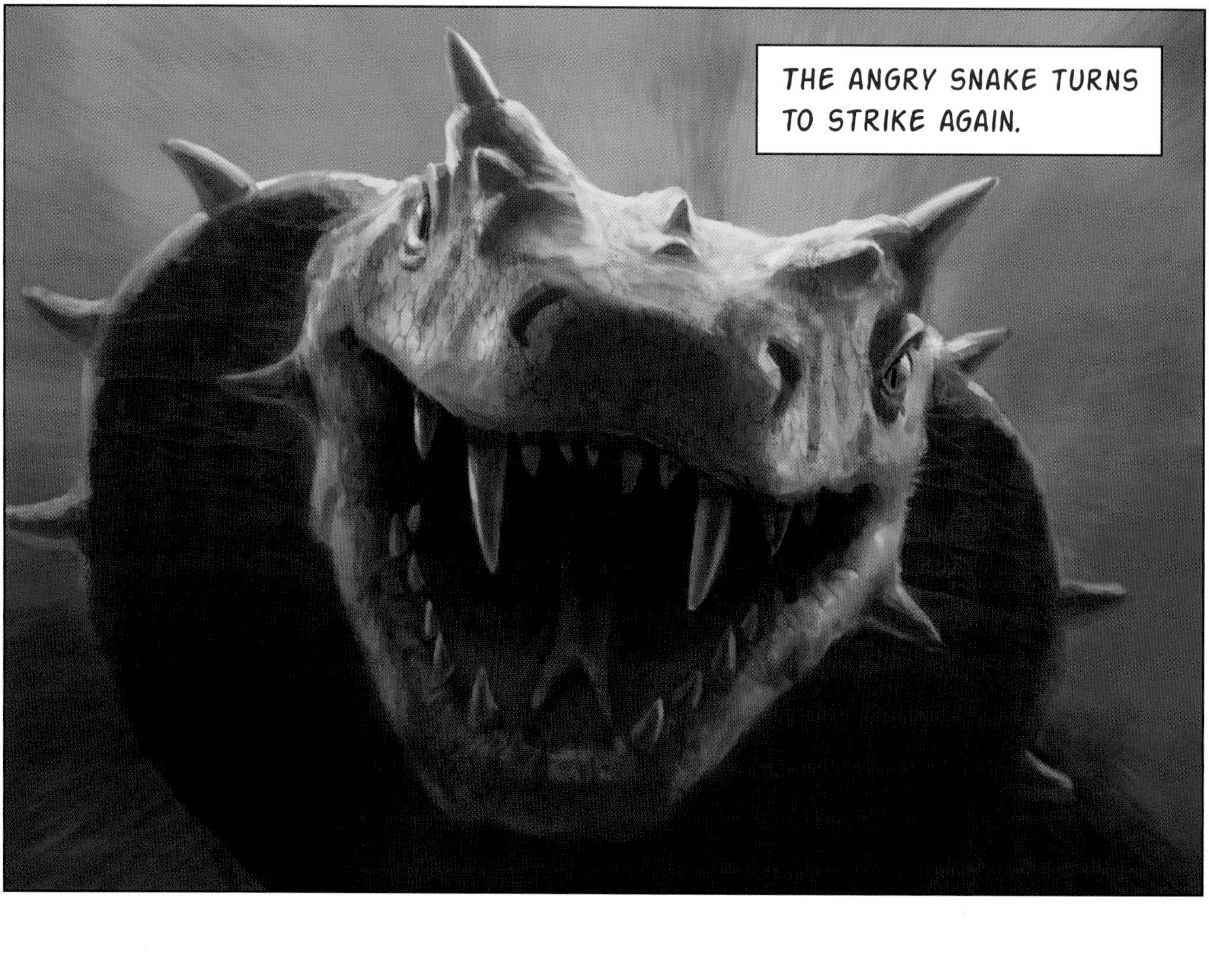
THE ANGRY SNAKE TURNS TO STRIKE AGAIN.

CAPTAIN RAPTOR STEADIES HIS WEAPON AND **FIRES**. THE LASER STREAM **BLASTS** INTO THE BEAST'S MOUTH. ONE OF ITS POISON FANGS IS KNOCKED OUT AND GOES SPINNING INTO THE JUNGLE.

COBRASAURUS SLINKS BACK INTO THE TREES, **WHINING** LIKE A SICK PUPPY.

"NEXT TIME KEEP YOUR FANGS TO YOURSELF!"

HIGHER AND HIGHER THE CAPTAIN CLIMBS.

HE FINALLY REACHES THE MOUTH OF AN ENORMOUS CAVE.

"THE SCIENTISTS' DISTRESS SIGNAL IS COMING FROM INSIDE THE CAVE, CAPTAIN," RADIOS SPIKEBACK.

CAPTAIN RAPTOR STEPS INTO THE MOUTH OF THE FORBIDDING CAVE AND MAKES HIS WAY THROUGH A DARK TUNNEL.

THE PATH ENDS, AND THE CAPTAIN FINDS HIMSELF ON THE EDGE OF A **LAVA LAKE.**

THROUGH THE HAZE OF STEAM, CAPTAIN RAPTOR CAN JUST MAKE OUT THE SCIENTISTS, TRAPPED ON WHAT IS LEFT OF A RESEARCH PLATFORM. BUBBLING LAVA RISES ALL AROUND THEM.

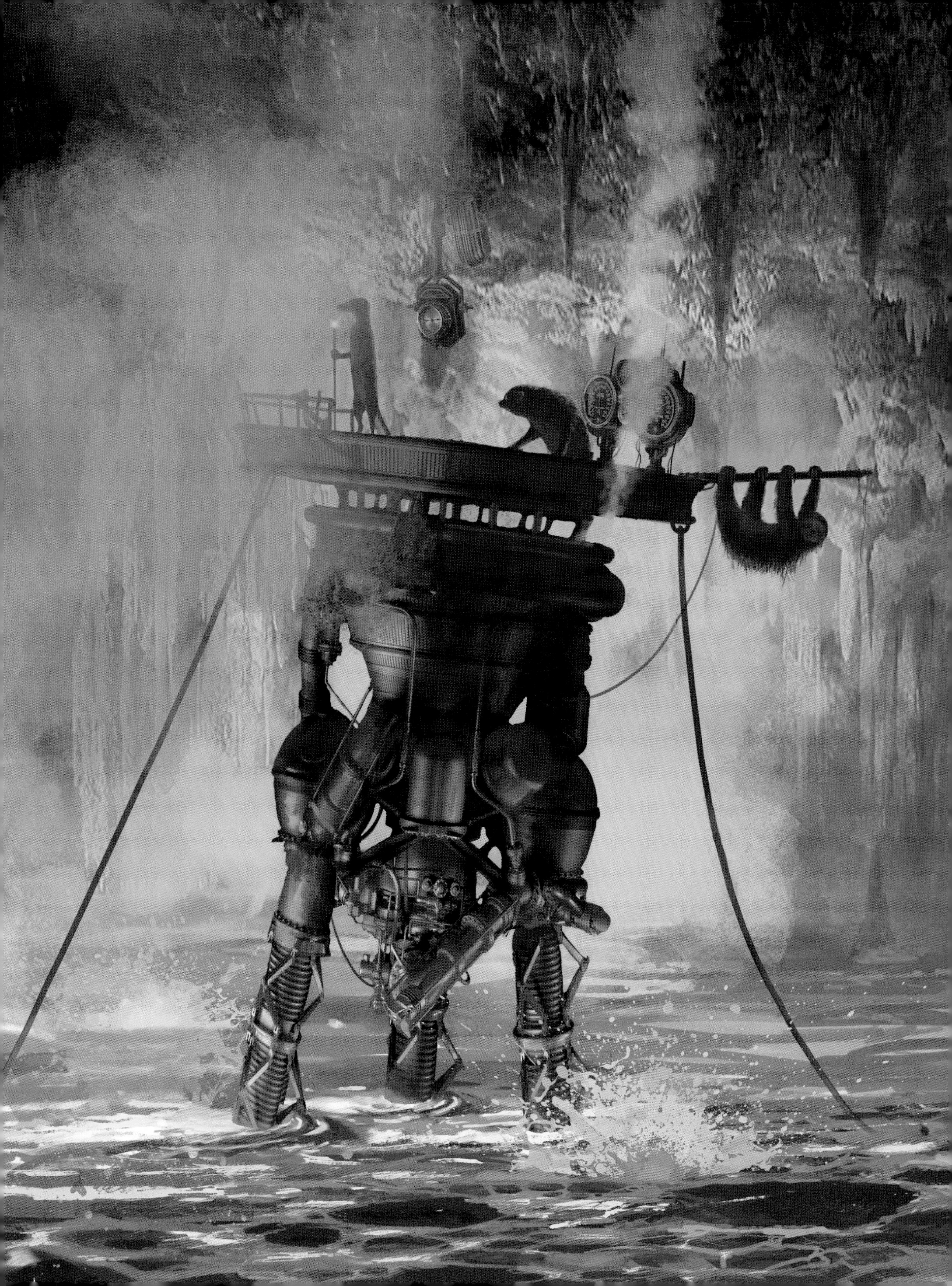

HIGH ABOVE, SOMETHING IS WATCHING.

THE RADIO SQUAWKS AGAIN. "CAPTAIN, THE MAMMALIAN SPACESHIP HAS LANDED. COMMANDER BROCK IS ON HIS WAY."

"THIS VOLCANO IS **GOING TO BLOW!**" RESPONDS CAPTAIN RAPTOR. "BE READY TO LEAVE ON MY SIGNAL!"

CAPTAIN RAPTOR FIRES A GRAPPLING HOOK ACROSS THE LAVA PIT.

HAND OVER HAND HE CROSSES THE CABLE.

"PLEASE," SAYS ONE OF THE SCIENTISTS, BARELY ABOVE A WHISPER. "WE MUST SAVE THE RESEARCH DATA. IT COULD MEAN LIFE OR DEATH FOR OUR HOME WORLD."

UNSEEN IN THE DARKNESS ABOVE, THE WATCHER BEGINS TO DESCEND.

SLOWLY, PAINFULLY, THE BRAVE CAPTAIN STARTS BACK ACROSS WITH THE SCIENTISTS. THE CABLE STRAINS UNDER THEIR WEIGHT.

AN UNFAMILIAR VOICE CRACKLES OVER THE RADIO. "HOLD ON, GOOD CAPTAIN— I'M ALMOST THERE!"

THE BEAST SILENTLY GLIDES LOWER AND LOWER.

VULTUROUS!

THE MASSIVE BIRD OF PREY SCREAMS AND DIVES FOR ITS NEXT MEAL.

IS *THIS* THE END OF CAPTAIN RAPTOR?

SUDDENLY A **BLAST** FROM A LASER CANNON SHOOTS OUT FROM DEEP IN THE TUNNEL.

THE MONSTER TIPS TO ITS SIDE, ITS ENORMOUS WING **SLICING** THE CABLE.

CAPTAIN RAPTOR **FALLS** FROM VIEW JUST AS COMMANDER BROCK REACHES THE EDGE.

"CAPTAIN, **CAN YOU HEAR ME?** ARE YOU THERE?" YELLS THE COMMANDER.

FROM BELOW HE HEARS A VOICE. "I COULD USE A HAND HERE, COMMANDER. THIS LUGGAGE ISN'T GETTING ANY LIGHTER."

COMMANDER BROCK PULLS THE CAPTAIN AND HIS CARGO TO SAFETY.

TOGETHER THEY **RACE THROUGH THE TUNNEL,** THE SCIENTISTS JUST BARELY ABLE TO SUPPORT THEIR OWN WEIGHT.

DOWN THE MOUNTAIN AND THROUGH THE JUNGLE THEY STAGGER. THE GROUND HEAVES, AND MOUNT BLEAK ERUPTS WITH A THUNDEROUS ROAR. GLOBS OF MOLTEN LAVA **CRASH** ALL AROUND THEM.

CAPTAIN RAPTOR LEADS THE WAY BACK TO THE SPACESHIPS, WHICH RUMBLE IN ANTICIPATION OF BLASTOFF.

"CAPTAIN, I SUGGEST YOU HURRY UP," URGES PROFESSOR ANGLEOPTEROUS.

"THE PLANET'S INSTABILITY IS INCREASING. IT CAN'T HOLD TOGETHER MUCH LONGER."

"I HEAR YOU, PROFESSOR. IS YOUR NEW SHIELDING SYSTEM READY?" ASKS THE CAPTAIN.

"I'M ON TEST NUMBER 232, CAPTAIN, BUT I THINK I'VE GOT MOST OF THE BUGS WORKED OUT THIS TIME."

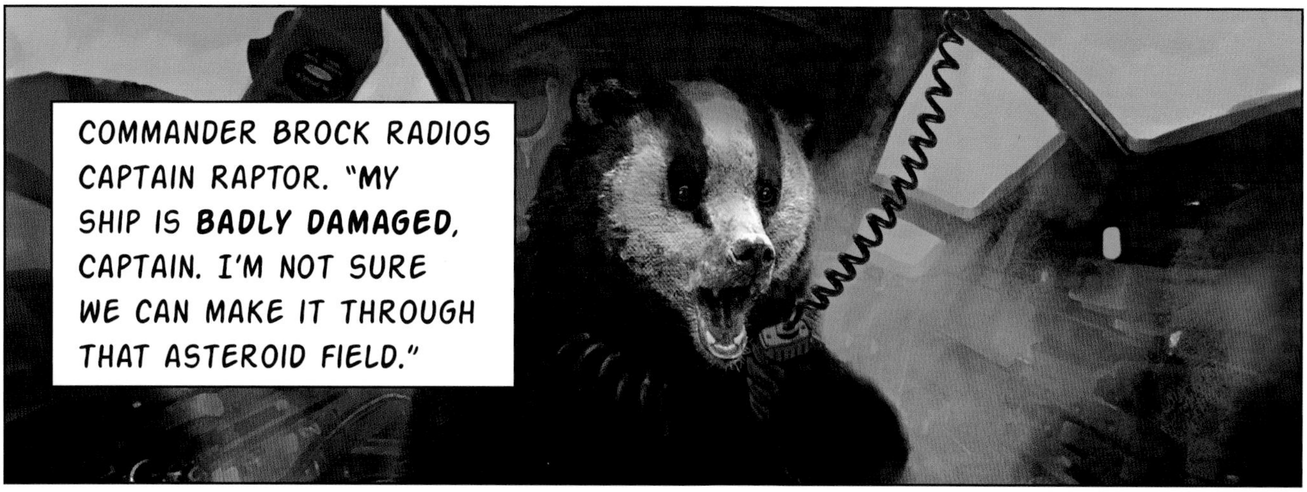
COMMANDER BROCK RADIOS CAPTAIN RAPTOR. "MY SHIP IS **BADLY DAMAGED**, CAPTAIN. I'M NOT SURE WE CAN MAKE IT THROUGH THAT ASTEROID FIELD."

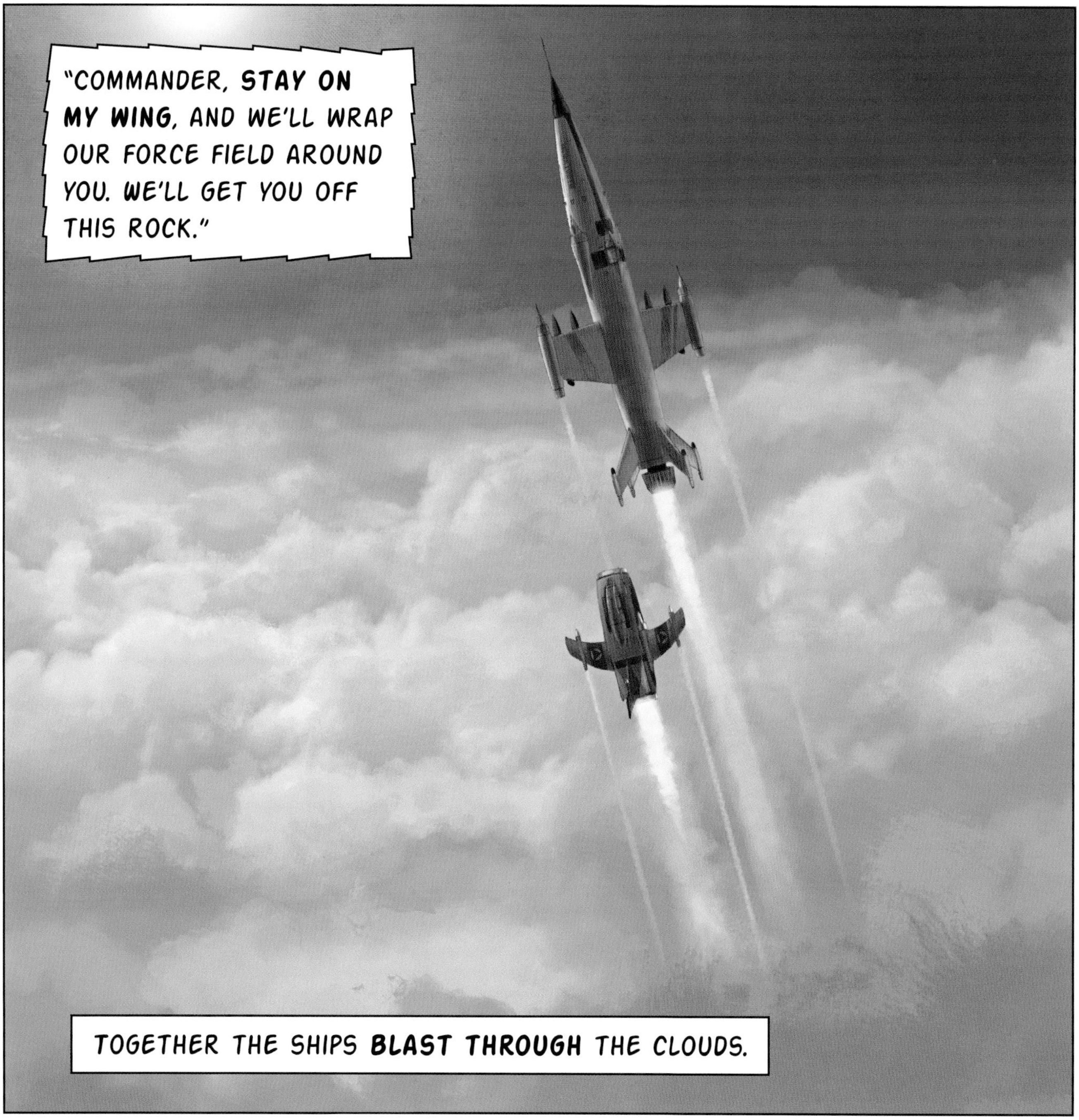
"COMMANDER, **STAY ON MY WING**, AND WE'LL WRAP OUR FORCE FIELD AROUND YOU. WE'LL GET YOU OFF THIS ROCK."
TOGETHER THE SHIPS **BLAST THROUGH** THE CLOUDS.

THREETOE PILOTS THE *MEGATOOTH* BETWEEN
ASTEROIDS, NARROWLY AVOIDING COLLISIONS.
BUT WHEN THEY REACH THE OUTER EDGE OF
THE PLANET'S ATMOSPHERE, THE FULL FORCE
OF THE **NIGHTMARE** HITS THEM.

"**DEPLOY THE SHIELD**, PROFESSOR!" SHOUTS CAPTAIN
RAPTOR OVER THE ROAR OF THE ENGINES. THE SHIELD
BLOCKS THE SMALLER FLAMING ROCKS, BUT THE
LARGER ONES **CRASH THROUGH.**

THE TWO SHIPS TAKE A TERRIBLE BEATING.

COULD *THIS* BE THE END OF CAPTAIN RAPTOR?

CAPTAIN RAPTOR GRABS THE WEAPONS CONTROLS. "COMMANDER BROCK, LET'S **BLOW A HOLE** IN ANYTHING THAT GETS IN OUR WAY!"

CANNON FIRE AND TORPEDO BLASTS **LIGHT UP** SPACE LIKE EXPLODING STARS. FINALLY THE TWO SHIPS ARE CLEAR OF DANGER.

AS THE SHIPS RACE AWAY FROM PYROS PRIME, THE PLANET **EXPLODES** BEHIND THEM.

"CAPTAIN RAPTOR, THANK YOU," RADIOS COMMANDER BROCK. "THE SCIENTISTS YOU RESCUED HAVE VITAL INFORMATION THAT WILL KEEP OUR PLANET SAFE FROM SUCH A FATE. WE ARE IN YOUR DEBT."

"YOU'RE WELCOME, COMMANDER BROCK. OH, AND THANK YOU FOR THE LIFT WHEN I NEEDED IT."

SUDDENLY COMMUNICATIONS SPECIALIST SPIKEBACK RACES ONTO THE COMMAND DECK. "CAPTAIN, THE PRESIDENT OF JURASSICA IS CALLING. **ALERT LEVEL ONE!** THE EMERGENCY BEACON ON PLANET SETI BETA SIX HAS GONE OFF. THE SETTLERS THERE NEED OUR HELP!"

"NEVER A DULL MOMENT," SAYS CAPTAIN RAPTOR. "UNTIL WE MEET AGAIN, COMMANDER . . .

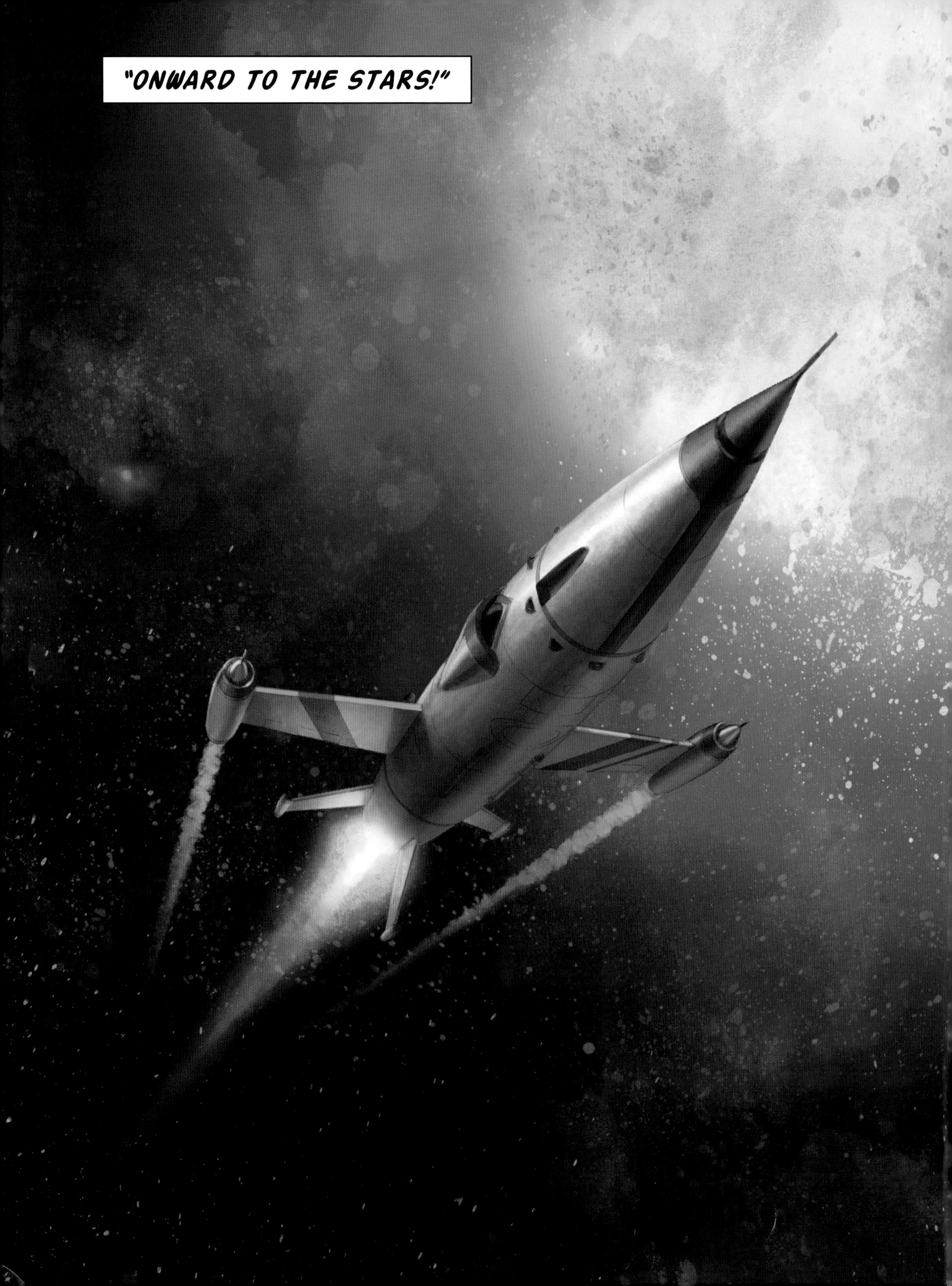
"ONWARD TO THE STARS!"

THIS BOOK IS FOR ALL THOSE FOLKS WHO, LIKE ME, LOVE SCI-FI, SCIENCE,
AND THE COLLECTIVE JOY OF ALL OUR VERY HUMAN, IMAGINATIVE DREAMS.
MOST OF ALL THIS BOOK IS FOR PAT O'BRIEN, A TERRIFIC ILLUSTRATOR AND
BRILLIANT FELLOW. THANK YOU, PAT.—K. O'M.

TO ALEX, IN SO MANY WAYS.—P. O'B.

TEXT COPYRIGHT © 2018 BY KEVIN O'MALLEY AND PATRICK O'BRIEN
ILLUSTRATIONS COPYRIGHT © 2018 BY PATRICK O'BRIEN
ALL RIGHTS RESERVED, INCLUDING THE RIGHT OF REPRODUCTION IN WHOLE OR IN PART IN ANY FORM.
CHARLESBRIDGE AND COLOPHON ARE REGISTERED TRADEMARKS OF CHARLESBRIDGE PUBLISHING, INC.

AT THE TIME OF PUBLICATION, ANY URLS PRINTED IN THIS BOOK WERE ACCURATE AND ACTIVE. CHARLESBRIDGE
AND THE AUTHORS ARE NOT RESPONSIBLE FOR THE CONTENT OR ACCESSIBILITY OF ANY URL.

PUBLISHED BY CHARLESBRIDGE
85 MAIN STREET
WATERTOWN, MA 02472
(617) 926-0329
WWW.CHARLESBRIDGE.COM

LIBRARY OF CONGRESS CATALOGING-IN-PUBLICATION DATA
NAMES: O'MALLEY, KEVIN, 1961– AUTHOR. | O'BRIEN, PATRICK, 1960– AUTHOR, ILLUSTRATOR.
TITLE: CAPTAIN RAPTOR AND THE PERILOUS PLANET/KEVIN O'MALLEY AND PATRICK O'BRIEN;
    ILLUSTRATED BY PATRICK O'BRIEN.
DESCRIPTION: WATERTOWN, MA: CHARLESBRIDGE, [2018] | SUMMARY: CAPTAIN RAPTOR AND THE CREW OF THE
    MEGATOOTH RUSH TO HELP RESCUE SCIENTISTS FROM THE PLANET MAMMALIA WHO ARE TRAPPED ON PYROS
    PRIME, AN UNSTABLE PLANET WITH EXPLODING VOLCANOES.
IDENTIFIERS: LCCN 2017028986 (PRINT) | LCCN 2017047184 (EBOOK) | ISBN 9781632896544 (EBOOK) | ISBN
    9781632896551 (EBOOK PDF) | ISBN 9781580898096 (REINFORCED FOR LIBRARY USE)
SUBJECTS: LCSH: DINOSAURS—JUVENILE FICTION. | RESCUES—JUVENILE FICTION. | LIFE ON OTHER PLANETS—
    JUVENILE FICTION. | SCIENCE FICTION. | CYAC: SCIENCE FICTION. | DINOSAURS—FICTION. | RESCUES—FICTION.
    | LIFE ON OTHER PLANETS—FICTION. | LCGFT: SCIENCE FICTION. | ACTION AND ADVENTURE FICTION.
CLASSIFICATION: LCC PZ7.0526 (EBOOK) | LCC PZ7.0526 CAP 2018 (PRINT) | DDC [E]–DC23
LC RECORD AVAILABLE AT HTTPS://LCCN.LOC.GOV/2017028986

PRINTED IN CHINA
(HC) 10 9 8 7 6 5 4 3 2 1

ILLUSTRATIONS DONE DIGITALLY
DISPLAY TYPE SET IN FEDORA OUTLINE SHADOW BY SHYFOUNDRY AND KENYAN COFFEE BY TYPODERMIC FONTS INC.
TEXT TYPE SET IN ACTION MAN BY ICONIAN FONTS/SHYFONTS TYPE FOUNDRY
COLOR SEPARATIONS BY COLOURSCAN PRINT CO PTE LTD, SINGAPORE
PRINTED BY 1010 PRINTING INTERNATIONAL LIMITED IN HUIZHOU, GUANGDONG, CHINA
PRODUCTION SUPERVISION BY BRIAN G. WALKER

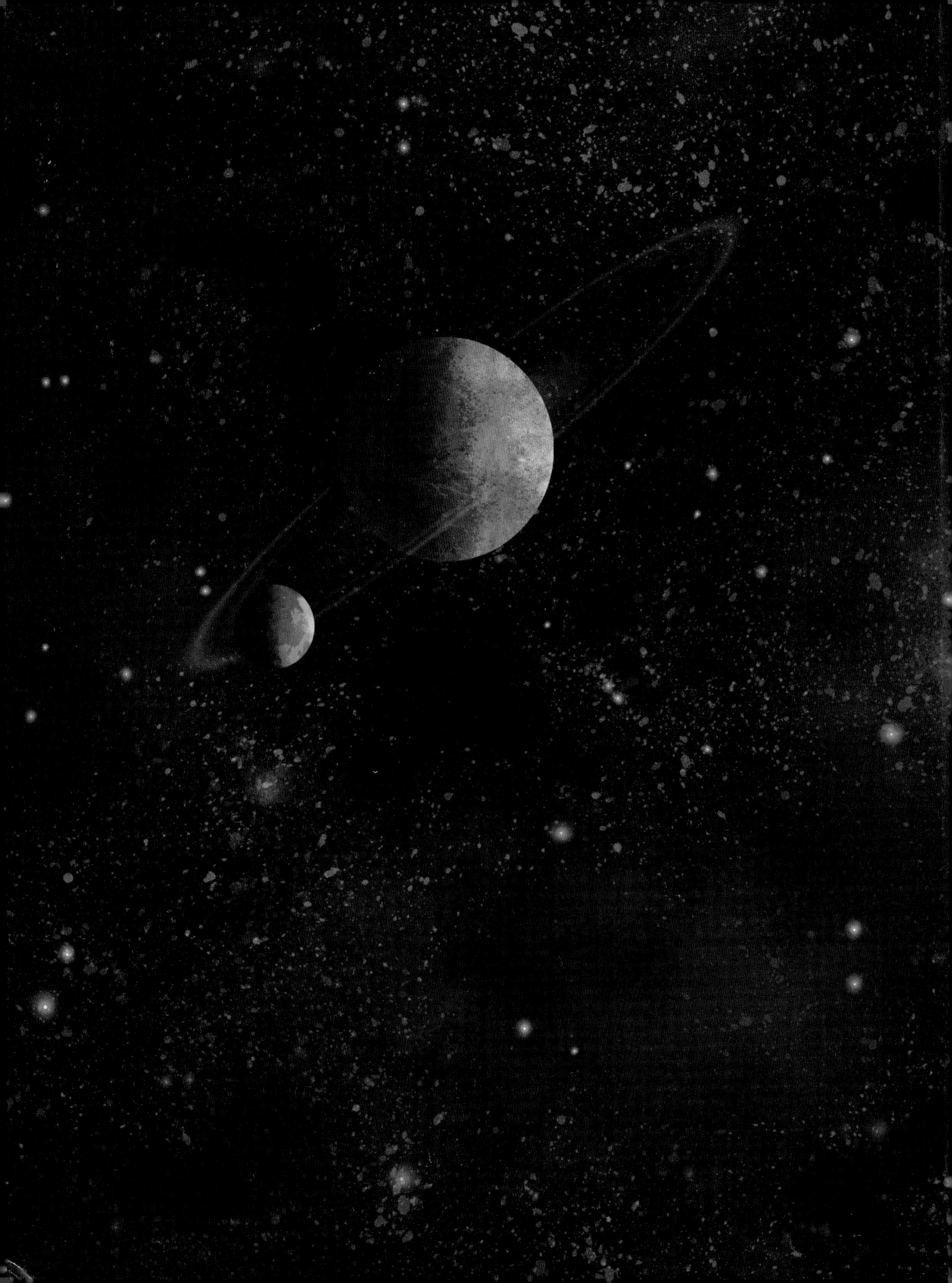